The Haunted Halloween Party

By Gail Herman
Illustrated by Duendes del Sur

SCHOLASTIC INC.
New York   Toronto   London   Auckland   Sydney
Mexico City   New Delhi   Hong Kong   Buenos Aires

ISBN 0-439-78811-0

20 19 18 17 16 15 14   40   12/0

Designed by Michael Massen

Printed in the U.S.A.
First printing, September 2006

It was Halloween night. Scooby-Doo and Shaggy were chowing at the Coolsville Pizza Joint.

Trick-or-treaters peeked inside. Scooby and Shaggy jumped.

"Like, Halloween is scary!" Shaggy said. "We're going to stay here all night long. Right, Scoob?"

"Right, Raggy."

5

"You can't do that," said Fred. He had come into the pizza place with Velma and Daphne. "The whole gang is invited to a Halloween party."

Go outside? On Halloween?
"Ro ray!" Scooby shook his head.
Shaggy ordered another pie.
Then Daphne showed him the invitation.
"Hot dogs! Hamburgers! Spaghetti and
neatballs! Fries!" read Shaggy.
"And *rizza*!" Scooby added.

7

"We'll go!" said Shaggy. "But we have to finish this pizza first."

"Meet us at the party!" Velma told them. "It's at the third house on Green Street."

Seconds later, Shaggy and Scooby
were done. They left the restaurant. The
streets were dark. A cold wind blew.
   "Nothing to be afraid of, good buddy,"
Shaggy said cheerfully.

"No trick-or-treaters here!" Shaggy
squinted at a street sign. "Third Street."
Shaggy and Scooby walked down the
block.

"We're here! The green house on Third
Street."

Shaggy and Scooby stared at the house. Weeds covered the front yard. The shutters hung from their hinges. Shaggy laughed. "Like, wow! The people who live here made the place look haunted."

"Don't trip on that gravestone!" Shaggy told Scooby. "It's a stage prop!"
Shaggy and Scooby stumbled up the old stone steps.

"Hello? Rello?" Shaggy and Scooby called.
No one answered. They stepped into the living room. Cobwebs hung from the ceiling.

"Great party decorations," said Shaggy. "Everyone must be upstairs."

Creak! Shaggy and Scooby hurried up the steps. On the second floor they looked around.

14

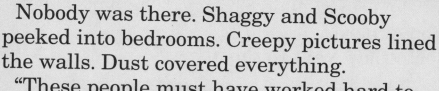

Nobody was there. Shaggy and Scooby peeked into bedrooms. Creepy pictures lined the walls. Dust covered everything.

"These people must have worked hard to make the whole place look so scary!" said Shaggy.

"Next floor!" said Shaggy. "The party's got to be there."

Up they went to the attic.

It was empty.
A large, long box stood in a corner.
"Like, this is one weird party," said Shaggy.
"There are no guests! And no food!"

"It's a coffin!" Shaggy cried. "And something just escaped!"

19

Scooby's knees knocked with fright. Shaggy's hair stood on end.

"Like, the party's over, good buddy!" Shaggy whispered. "This is a *real* haunted house."

"And Red . . . Relma . . . Raphne . . . ?" whimpered Scooby.

". . . must be goners!" Shaggy finished.

21

Whoosh! The attic door slammed shut. Shaggy rushed to open it. He couldn't. There was no knob.

"We should have stayed at the Pizza Joint!" Shaggy sobbed. "Help!"

"Relp!" called Scooby.

"Hey!" a voice called from outside. Shaggy and Scooby looked out the window.

It was Fred!

"You guys are in the wrong house!" he said. "The party is over here at the third house on Green Street, not the *green* house on *Third* Street!"

23

"Zoinks!" Shaggy cried. "Like, Fred is okay! We're the ones in trouble!"

Shaggy and Scooby held each other tight.

Thud!

Something was coming up the stairs.

THUD! THUD!

Closer and closer.

The door swung open.

"Hi, guys!" said Velma. The rest of the
gang was behind her.

Bang!

The door slammed shut.

"W-w-wait," Shaggy spluttered. "We've got to get out of here. That's a coffin. There's a grave in the front yard. And this place is haunted."

A dark shape scuttled past.

"See?" Shaggy asked.

"It's just a cute little mouse," said Daphne. Velma pushed the door. It swung right open. "And the coffin? Why, that's just an old moving crate," Fred said.

Velma led Scooby and Shaggy outside.

"This house hasn't been lived in for a while," Velma explained. "See. . . ."

Velma brushed weeds off the sign. It read: FOR SALE

"Now let's all go to the real party!" Fred said. They crossed the street. "Like, this is more like it!" said Shaggy.

"Boo!" said a friendly ghost.
"Not boo . . ." Shaggy said.

"Scooby-Dooby-BOO!"